JUST LIKE
BOSSY BEAR

DAVID HORVATH

Disney · Hyperion Books
New York

To Mina

Printed in Singapore
First Edition
10 9 8 7 6 5 4 3 2 1
Library of Congress Cataloging-in-Publication Data on file.
ISBN 978-1-4231-1097-2
Reinforced binding
Visit www.hyperionbooksforchildren.com

Bossy Bear is very bossy.

He likes things a certain way—his way.

Turtle is Bossy Bear's best friend.

They do everything together.

Turtle wants to be just like Bossy Bear.

Bossy says . . .
GIMME THAT!

Then, one day . . .

READ TO ME!

I WANT *ALL* THE CANDY!!!!

**Bossy Bear realized that
Turtle had become very bossy . . .**

JUST LIKE BOSSY BEAR!

Then Bossy Bear had an idea.

He would set a good example.

HAVE A GOOD MORNING!

WATCH YOUR STEP!

EAT YOUR VEGGIES!!!

SLEEP TIGHT!
DON'T LET THE BEDBUGS BITE!

HAVE A GREAT TRIP!!!

Would it work?

YOU HAD BETTER . . .

. . . **have a nice day.**